Story Time with Signs & Rhymes

Four Seasons! Five Senses!
Sign Language for the Seasons and the Senses

by Dawn Babb Prochovnic
illustrated by Stephanie Bauer

Content Consultant:
Lora Heller, MS, MT-BC, LCAT
and Founding Director of Baby Fingers LLC

magic

visit us at www.abdopublishing.com

For my five favorite ASL teachers: Lora Heller, Nellie Edge, Monta Briant, Penny Warner, and Rachel Coleman—DP
For our own little Penguin bottom, Figgy—SB

Printed in the United States of America, North Mankato, Minnesota.
102011
012012
This book contains at least 10% recycled materials.

♻ Written by Dawn Babb Prochovnic
Illustrations by Stephanie Bauer
Edited by Stephanie Hedlund and Rochelle Baltzer
Cover and interior layout and design by Neil Klinepier

Story Time with Signs & Rhymes provides an introduction to ASL vocabulary through stories that are written and structured in English. ASL is a separate language with its own structure. Just as there are personal and regional variations in spoken and written languages, there are similar variations in sign language.

Library of Congress Cataloging-in-Publication Data

Prochovnic, Dawn Babb.
  Four seasons! five senses! : sign language for the seasons and senses / by Dawn Babb Prochovnic ; illustrated by Stephanie Bauer.
      p. cm. -- (Story time with signs & rhymes)
  Summary: Playful stories in simple rhymes introduce the American Sign Language signs for the seasons and different senses.
  ISBN 978-1-61641-836-6
  1. American Sign Language--Juvenile fiction. 2. Stories in rhyme. 3. Seasons--Juvenile fiction. 4. Senses and sensa-tion--Juvenile fiction. [1. Seasons--Fiction. 2. Senses and sensation--Fiction. 3. Sign language. 4. Stories in rhyme.] I. Bauer, Stephanie, ill. II. Title. III. Series: Story time with signs & rhymes.
  PZ10.4.P76Fo 2012
  [E]--dc23   2011027064

Alphabet Handshapes

American Sign Language (ASL) is a visual language that uses handshapes, movements, and facial expressions. Sometimes people spell English words by making the handshape for each letter in the word they want to sign. This is called fingerspelling. The pictures below show the handshapes for each letter in the manual alphabet.

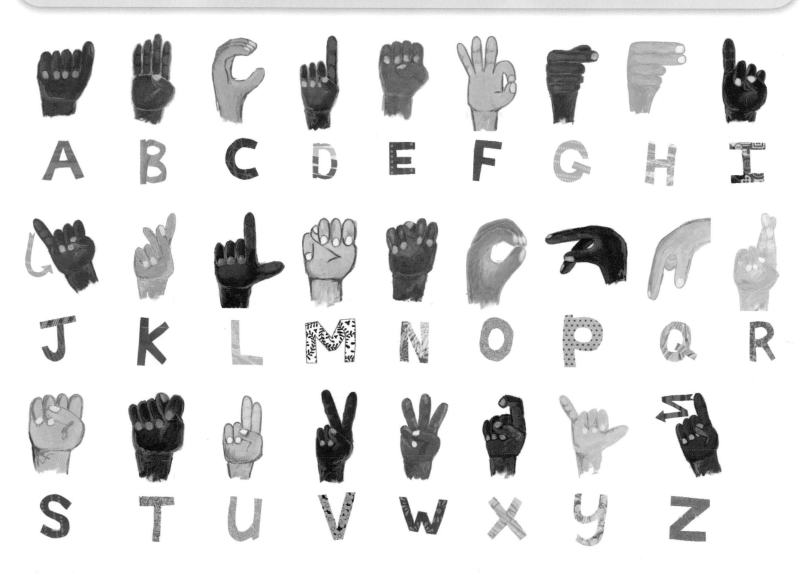

ACHOO!

It is **winter!**
I see a sled. I see some skis.
I hear a sniffle and a sneeze.

4

winter

My hands **feel** cold. As cold as ice.
My nose smells peppermint and spice.

feel

I love the **taste** of chicken soup on a cozy winter day.

taste

It is spring!
I see pink blooms on bright green trees.
I hear the buzz of bumblebees.

spring

11

I feel wet puddles with my feet.
I **smell** the air. It's fresh and sweet.

12

smell

I love the **taste** of homemade bread on a rainy springtime day.

taste

It is summer!
I see the sun. I see the shade.
I **hear** a friend shout, "Lemonade!"

hear

I **feel** warm sand between my toes.
I smell the sunscreen on my nose.

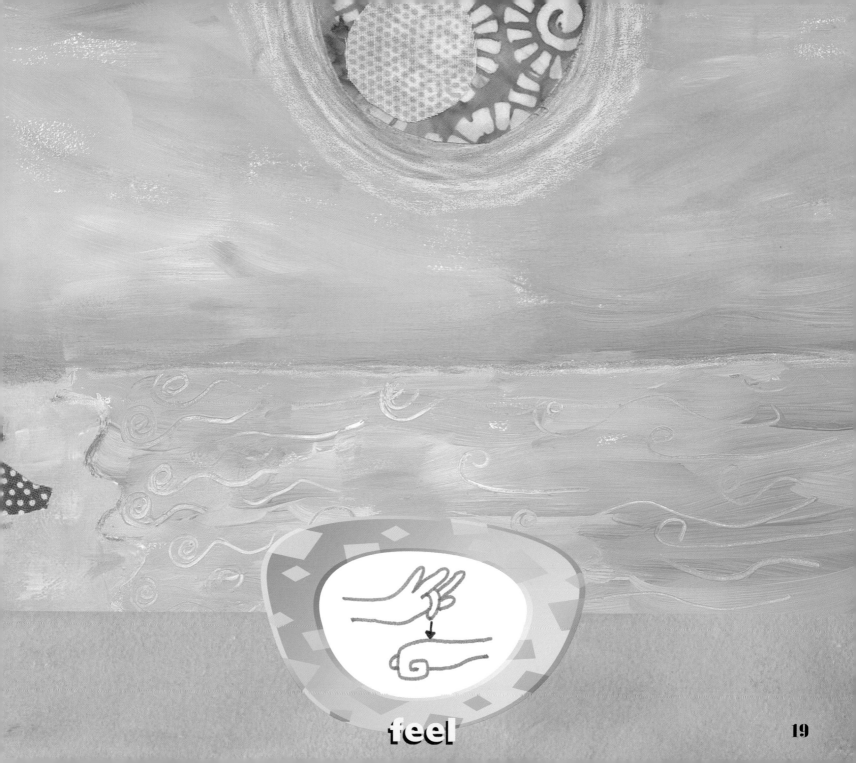

feel

I love the taste of berry jam on a lazy **summer** day.

20

summer

It is autumn!
I see red leaves. I see a ghoul.
I hear my mom say, "Time for school."

22

SCHOOL

see

I feel the wind against my face.
I **smell** a smoky fireplace.

smell

I love the taste of pumpkin pie on a chilly **autumn** day.

26

autumn

American Sign Language Glossary

autumn: Hold your left arm in front of your body with your elbow pointing slightly down and your hand near your shoulder. Now brush your left elbow with the side of your right hand a couple of times. The palm of your right hand should be pointing down. It should look like leaves falling off the branch of a tree.

feel: *Use the sign for touch.* Hold your left arm in front of your body with your palm facing down. Now tap the back of your left hand a couple of times with the middle finger of your right "Five Hand." The palm of your right hand should be facing down, and the fingertip of your right middle finger should be pointing down.

hear: One way to make this sign is to make a "C Hand," but hold your fingers and thumb farther apart than usual. Put your hand near your ear like you are listening closely to what someone has to say. Another way to make this sign is to use your pointer finger to tap your ear a couple of times.

see: Use the middle finger of your "V Hand" to touch your cheekbone just below your eye. Your palm should be facing toward you. Now move your "V Hand" down and away from your face. Your middle finger should be pointing slightly toward you and your pointer finger should be pointing up.

smell: Brush the palm of your hand against the tip of your nose a couple of times. Your hand should move in an arc, up and away from your nose. It should look like you are moving the air in front of your nose to smell a fragrance.

spring: Make a "C" handshape with your left hand, but position it so your thumb and pointer finger are facing up and your pinkie finger is facing down. Now push your right flattened "O Hand" through your left "C Hand" then quickly open your right hand. The fingertips of your right hand should be pointing up and the palm of your right hand should be facing you. Repeat this movement a couple of times. It should look like plants are sprouting out of the ground.

summer: Hold your right pointer finger over your eyebrows with your palm facing down. Now slide your pointer finger across your forehead to the right ending with your pointer finger bent and your hand near the right side of your head. It should look like you are wiping sweat off of your forehead.

taste: Use the middle finger of your "Five Hand" to tap your lips a couple of times. Your other fingers should be pointing up.

winter: Many people use the sign for cold. Hold your "S Hands" in front of you with your palms facing each other. Now hunch your shoulders and move your fists in a tight up and down shivering motion. It should look like you are shivering. Some people make the sign for winter with "W Hands" instead of "S Hands."

Fun Facts about ASL

Most sign language dictionaries describe how a sign looks for a right-handed signer. If you are left-handed, you would modify the instructions so the signs feel more comfortable to you. For example, to sign *autumn*, a left-handed signer would brush the right elbow with the side of the left hand.

Facial expressions and body language are an important part of communicating in sign language. For example, to communicate that it is *very cold*, you would simply exaggerate the sign for *cold*. You could do this by scrunching your face to show that you are very cold and uncomfortable. You could also shiver your fists and hunch your shoulders more than usual.

Sometimes there is more than one sign for the same English word. For example, the sign for *smell* described in the glossary means a fragrant smell or the sense of smell. To sign that something smells stinky, you would use your pointer finger and thumb to plug your nose. Your palm should face down and your eyebrows should be lowered. It should look like you are plugging your nose because something smells bad.

Signing Activities

Guess My Season: This is a fun activity for partners. Write a poem or story about your favorite time of year. Be sure to include what you see, hear, feel, smell, and taste during that time of year. Read your poem or story to a partner and see if he or she can guess what season you had in mind. Your partner must make the sign for each season until it is guessed correctly. When your partner guesses correctly, switch roles.

Act Out!: This is a fun game for partners. Get some blank index cards and write the word for one of the five senses on three different cards. Leave the back of the cards blank. Repeat this process until you have three cards for each of the five senses. Shuffle the cards and put them facedown in a pile. The player who goes first takes a card from the pile and makes the sign for the word on the card. The partner must repeat this sign and make the sign for one of the four seasons. The player who goes first must act out a scene that includes elements for both words. For example, if the words signed were taste and winter, the player might pretend to taste a sip of hot cocoa, since hot cocoa is a common winter drink. When the first player finishes acting out the scene, switch roles. Continue taking turns until all the cards have been used.

Additional Resources

Further Reading

Coleman, Rachel. *Once Upon a Time* (Signing Time DVD, Series 2, Volume 11). Two Little Hands Productions, 2008.

Edge, Nellie. *ABC Phonics: Sing, Sign, and Read!* Northlight Communications, 2010.

Heller, Lora. *Sign Language for Kids.* Sterling, 2004.

Valli, Clayton. *The Gallaudet Dictionary of American Sign Language.* Gallaudet University Press, 2005.

Web Sites

To learn more about ASL, visit ABDO Group online at **www.abdopublishing.com**. Web sites about ASL are featured on our Book Links page. These links are routinely monitored and updated to provide the most current information available.